The Orange Shoes

Trinka Hakes Noble ❧ Illustrated by Doris Ettlinger

For Carl and Eva Hakes
In loving memory.
There never were better parents than mine.

T.H.N.

To Pat McCarthy and Merial Cornell

D.E.

✃

Sleeping Bear Press™
310 North Main Street, Suite 300
Chelsea, MI 48118
www.sleepingbearpress.com

THOMSON
✶
GALE

© 2007 Thomson Gale, a part of the Thomson Corporation.
Thomson, Star Logo and Sleeping Bear Press are trademarks
and Gale is a registered trademark used herein under license.

Printed and bound in China.

First Edition

10 9 8 7 6 5 4 3 2 1

Library of Congress Cataloging-in-Publication Data

Noble, Trinka Hakes.
The orange shoes / written by Trinka Hakes Noble ; illustrated by Doris Ettlinger.
p. cm.
Summary: Delly Porter enjoys the feel of soft dirt beneath her feet as she walks to
and from school, but after a classmate makes her feel ashamed of having no shoes she
learns that her parents and others, too, see value in things that do not cost money.
ISBN 978-1-58536-277-6
ISBN 1-58536-277-8
[1. Shoes--Fiction. 2. Poverty--Fiction. 3. Family life--Fiction. 4. Artists--Fiction.
5. Schools--Fiction.] I. Ettlinger, Doris, ill. II. Title.

PZ7.N6715Ora 2007
[Fic]--dc22
2007006393

October's here and I still don't have new shoes. So I walk a mile to school in my bare feet. But that's fine with me because I love the feel of our dirt road under my feet; the sandy places and the dried mud places and the smooth places after the road scraper's gone through. I was happy going barefoot until one day …

… Prudy Winfield said only poor kids went barefoot, and come cold weather, I'd get frostbite and my toes would turn black and ugly and fall off. Then I couldn't walk to school so I'd get dumber and poorer. And if I had any kids, they'd get even dumber and poorer than me. That's what Prudy Winfield said.

Then one day our teacher, Miss Violet, made an announcement.

"Girls and boys," she smiled, "next week is our Harvest Festival and all your families are invited. We'll have our usual pumpkin carving and the Pumpkin Parade, but this year we're going to do something special. I'm asking the older students to put on a Shoebox Social to raise money for school art supplies."

I didn't know what a Shoebox Social was, but I knew about art because I'd been drawing ever since I could remember. True, I didn't have any real art supplies at home, but I had a stubby pencil I liked even though its eraser was missing, and I'd made my own sketchbook out of old envelopes. You just open them up flat and sew them together. There's a lot of good clean paper inside of used envelopes just waiting to be drawn on.

Since I didn't have an eraser, I'd practice drawing in my head first, and that made my drawings real works of art. So not having an eraser was a good thing, just like not wearing shoes is a good thing or how else are you going to know how soft and smooth and silky dirt is?

Now Prudy Winfield had forty-eleven pencils with fat pink erasers just oozing out of her neat wooden pencil case, which was right under my nose since we shared a desk. And she had lots of shoes, too. Today she had on shiny black patent leathers.

"Miss Violet, what's a Shoebox Social?" Prudy asked as she slid her toe into a patch of sunlight to make her shoe dazzle.

"Well, Prudence," answered Miss Violet, who always used our real names, "it's when a beautifully decorated box is packed with a supper and auctioned off to the highest bidder; then the money goes for a good cause. But our Shoebox Social will be more fun because each of you will stand behind the curtain when your box is up for auction, and stick out just your shoe so the families have a clue as to who you are. Then you will eat dinner with whomever buys your box."

"Now I'm counting on you older students to work hard on your boxes," Miss Violet continued, "and your mothers can help with the food."

Prudy Winfield pointed her toe like a ballet dancer and gloated, "I think I'll get a new pair of shoes for the Shoebox Social. What about you, Delly?"

Then she leaned toward me and jeered, "Gonna wash your feet for the occasion?"

Right then something lurched in the pit of my stomach, shot up to my chest, and clutched tight at my heart. It started to hurt and it didn't let up for the whole day, not even when Miss Violet asked me sweetly, "Adella, would you clean the chalk erasers today?"

That night at supper we had my favorite—
cornmeal mush drizzled with warm maple
syrup. It made me feel a bit better, so I
decided to tell Momma and Daddy about
the Shoebox Social. Then I was going to
ask for a new pair of shoes but Daddy
started talking about tires for his truck.

"The old ones can't be patched anymore,"
he said looking seriously at Momma.

"But Delly needs new shoes before winter,
her being the oldest," Momma fretted.
All I had to do was look at my four younger
brothers and sisters and see all my old shoes.

"But if I can't get to work we can't buy
groceries," said Daddy. "Now which is more
important, food on the table or new shoes
on Delly's feet?" Momma didn't answer.
I guess Daddy's truck needed new shoes
more than I did.

After supper I told Momma about the
Shoebox Social and in the night I heard
their voices floating softly up the stairs
and on Saturday we went to town.

On Main Street was Sussman's Department Store which sold just about everything including shoes and tires. And right there in the front window, perched on a pedestal, were the most beautiful pair of girl's shoes I'd ever seen … and they were orange … a creamy orange like the soft side of a pumpkin where it lay in the garden dirt. I knew they'd fit, yet they'd never be mine. Too much money. But the looking was free.

Then Daddy came along. "What's got your interest there, Delly?" he asked. I just pointed to those soft orange shoes. Then Daddy looked away, far far away.

I don't know how Daddy did it, but the next morning those orange shoes were by my bed. I slipped them on, fastened each strap with a pearl button and flew downstairs.

"Daddy, how'd you ever? What about your new tires?" I squealed.

"I got by with just two new ones so there was some leftover money," he said. Then he handed me my old brown shoes that he'd patched up with the old tires and beamed at my new orange shoes. "I guess the Porter family will be going to the Shoebox Social on Friday night."

There never was a better Daddy than mine!

On Monday morning I did something I shouldn't have. I took my new orange shoes to school, just to show the girls, and only at recess. So I hid them under a hazelnut bush at the edge of the schoolyard.

At recess, the boys ran to play baseball in Elder Browning's hayfield, while the girls stayed to play on the swings. I quickly slipped on my orange shoes and ran to the swings in a flash … an orange flash!

"My Daddy got them for me," I blurted out happily as the girls crowded around me. I thought my new shoes would make them happy, too, but they didn't even smile.

Suddenly Prudy Winfield ground her foot right down on my toe. "Dirt-poor Delly Porter can't have better shoes than us!" she sneered. "Yeah," someone hissed and my other toe got stomped. I tried to get away but they chased after me, scraping and scuffing and scratching my new shoes 'til one pearl button flew off. Finally Miss Violet rang the bell to line up.

By the time I'd hidden my orange shoes and ran to the end of the line, my heart was hurting so bad I thought it'd never stop.

It was a long walk home from school that afternoon. I sneaked upstairs so Momma wouldn't see my wrecked shoes. I stared at them, every dirty crack, scrape, scratch, and scuff mark, 'til they blurred into tears. My beautiful orange shoes were ruined. Everything was ruined. Everything.

So I did the only thing that ever made me feel better. I reached for my envelope sketchbook to draw. But when I closed my eyes to draw first in my head, all I could see were my ruined shoes. So then I clenched my teeth and squeezed my eyes tighter and tighter until they stung and all I saw was a greenish purplish-black.

When I opened my eyes things were out of focus. So I blinked and suddenly, right there on my shoes, just as clear as day, I saw a tiny vine in one of the cracks. Then one scratch looked like a leaf and a scuff mark looked like a pretty wild rose. Maybe, just maybe …

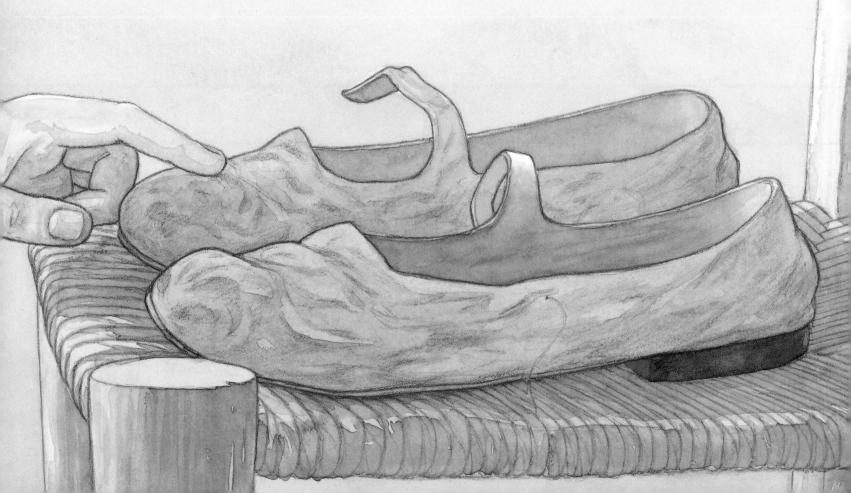

I rushed downstairs and shouted excitedly, "Momma, we got any paint?"

"I knew you'd be asking me that," Momma said quietly.

That stopped me cold in my tracks. Did Momma know what had happened?

"I knew a good artist like you would want to get started decorating your box for the Shoebox Social," Momma answered, handing me the brown shoe box she'd saved from Sussman's Department Store.

I don't know how Momma did it but she'd made little dishes of paint. There was red from beet juice and yellow from goldenrod blossoms and brownish-pink from onion skins and purple from turnip peelings. Then she'd made two brushes and a quill pen from turkey feathers.

"Momma, how'd you ever?" I exclaimed.

"It's not hard if you know where to look," she smiled, and I knew just what she meant.

There never was a better Momma than mine!

Every day after school, I painted pretty vines and flowers on my box, then painted the same designs on my shoes. By Friday they were a matched set except for the missing pearl button. But an artist knows where to look, so I ran out to our dirt road, and right there I spied a tiny white pebble shaped just like a little heart. I wound it in white thread and sewed it where the pearl button had been. There. Perfect.

But Momma and Daddy still didn't know what had happened, so I put my shoes in a sack, pretending I didn't want to get them dirty, and wore my patched-up shoes. It was a golden Indian summer evening, so we walked to the Harvest Festival to save gas.

Our schoolhouse was decorated with pumpkins, cornstalks, and bright autumn leaves. Miss Violet had strung a curtain across the front like a stage. Elder Browning brought gallons of fresh cider and plenty of pumpkins for everyone to carve, and Mrs. Browning carried in a huge platter of applesauce doughnuts.

Then Miss Violet hustled all the older girls and boys up behind the curtain and handed our boxes out to Elder Browning, our auctioneer, who lined them up. Then she lined us up, putting Prudy first and me last. No one noticed when I slipped on my newly painted orange shoes.

"Folks, this is for a good cause, so dig deep in your pockets," announced Elder Browning as he held up Prudy's pink polka-dotted box. "Who'll give me a quarter for this pretty box? Do I hear a quarter?"

Prudy inched her white patent leather pink-bowed shoe under the curtain and the bidding shot up 'til Elder Browning shouted, "Sold for one dollar and ninety cents!"

Prudy looked down her snooty nose at the rest of us as if to say, 'Let's see you top that!'

The next box brought 71 cents and the next one 53 cents and then only 35 cents and so on 'til Miss Violet nervously bit her lip as she calculated sums in her head.

Finally Elder Browning held up my box and gasped, "This one's a beauty, folks!" The room hushed.

Miss Violet looked at me, then at my shoes. "Oh, Adella," she sighed and lightly placed her hands on my shoulders as I slid my toe under the curtain.

In no time, the bidding raced to one dollar! Then one twenty-five! Miss Violet squeezed my shoulders. I inched my toe out some more and the bidding took off fast and furious ... one fifty, one seventy-five. Then two dollars. I'd passed Prudy!

Then two fifty, two eighty-five, all the way to two ninety! Elder Browning wiped his brow and panted, "Do I hear three? Any takers at three?" The room grew tense, silent. Folks held their breath. Three dollars was a fortune. "Last chance. Going once ... going twice ..."

Suddenly I heard my father speak in a strong sure voice. "I can manage three," he said, "because to me that box is priceless, just like the girl who painted it."

Elder Browning slammed down his gavel. "Sold to Mr. Porter, a man who knows what to value!" Then he opened the curtain and everyone applauded. As we stepped out, Miss Violet kept her hands on my shoulders and it felt like we were one person.

After we'd finished all the doughnuts, cider, and our box suppers, we carved the pumpkins. Then we had the Pumpkin Parade while Miss Violet and Elder Browning counted the money.

"If my pencilin' is up to snuff, I think we have the final tally, folks," announced Elder Browning. Then he handed the total to Miss Violet who looked straight at me and said importantly, "I'd like Adella Porter to come forward, please."

Miss Violet had me stand on a stool. It made me nervous standing so high in front of everyone, like I might tip over. She motioned for me to turn around on my toes so everyone could see my shoes and said, "Friends, this is why our school needs art supplies, for young artists like Adella."

I don't know what got into me, but right then I pointed my toe like a ballet dancer and stuck it right in Prudy Winfield's face … but just for a second.

"And I'm pleased to announce that we've collected a grand total of seven dollars and twelve cents!" Folks started to applaud, but Miss Violet put up her hand for silence. "And, because of Adella's artistic talents and her father's generosity, each student can have their very own paint set!"

All the kids jumped up and cheered while Momma and Daddy nodded their approval. Then I just grinned from ear to ear.

As we started to walk home down our dirt road, a harvest moon as big as a pumpkin rose over the cornfields. Suddenly Daddy pulled off his shoes and socks and sang out, "Last chance to go barefoot before winter sets in!"

So we all walked home barefoot, with Daddy laughing and Momma smiling and me leading the way through all the sandy places and the dried mud places and the smooth places after the road scraper's gone through. And for a second, I felt sad that poor Prudy Winfield would never know what going barefoot was like … but only for a second.

ML

5/08